THE DRAGONSITTER

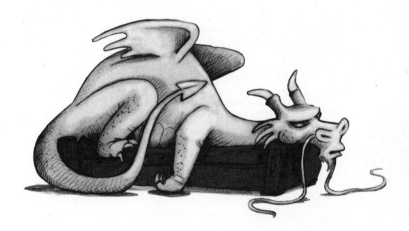

Josh Lacey

Illustrated by Garry Parsons

LITTLE, BROWN AND COMPANY
New York • Boston

Text copyright © 2012 by Josh Lacey
Illustrations copyright © 2012 by Garry Parsons
Text in excerpt from *The Dragonsitter Takes Off* copyright © 2013 by Josh Lacey
Illustrations in excerpt from *The Dragonsitter Takes Off* copyright © 2013 by Garry
Parsons

Little, Brown and Company

Hachette Book Group
1290 Avenue of the Americas, New York, NY 10104
Visit us at lb-kids.com

Little, Brown and Company is a division of Hachette Book Group, Inc.
The Little, Brown name and logo are trademarks of Hachette Book Group, Inc.

The publisher is not responsible for websites (or their content) that are not owned
by the publisher.

First U.S. Edition: September 2015
Originally published in Great Britain in 2012 by Andersen Press Limited

Library of Congress Control Number: 2015930244

ISBN 978-0-316-29896-4

10 9 8 7 6 5 4 3 2 1

RRD-C

Printed in the United States of America

THE DRAGONSITTER

Dear Uncle Morton,

You'd better get on a plane right now and come back here. Your dragon has eaten Jemima.

Emily loved that rabbit!

I know what you're thinking, Uncle Morton. We promised to look after your dragon for a whole week. I know we did. But you never said he would be like this.

Emily's in her bedroom now, crying so loudly the whole street must be able to hear.

Your dragon's sitting on the sofa, licking his claws, looking very pleased with himself.

If you don't come and collect him, Mom is going to phone the zoo. She says she doesn't know what else to do.

I don't want the dragon to live behind bars. I bet you don't, either. But I can't stop Mom. So please come and get him.

I'd better go now. I can smell burning.

Eddie

From: Edward Smith–Pickle

To: Morton Pickle

Date: Sunday, July 31

Subject: Your dragon

Attachments: Poopy shoes

Dear Uncle Morton,

I'm sorry for getting so angry when I wrote to you earlier, but your dragon is really irritating.

I hope you haven't changed your flight. If you have, you can change it back again. I persuaded Mom to give your dragon another chance.

Luckily, she didn't see him chasing Mrs. Kapelski's cats out of the yard.

Uncle M, I wish you'd told us a bit more about your dragon. You just handed him over and said he'd be fine and got back in your taxi to go to the airport. You didn't even tell us his name. And some instructions would have been helpful. Mom and I don't know anything about dragons. Emily says she does, but she's lying. She's only five and she doesn't know anything about anything.

For instance, what does he eat?

We looked for help on the Internet, but there was nothing useful.

One website said dragons eat only coal. Another said they prefer damsels in distress.

When I told Mom, she said, "Then I'd better look out, hadn't I?"

But your dragon doesn't seem so fussy. He eats just about anything. Rabbits, of course. And cold spaghetti. And sardines and baked beans and olives and apples and whatever else we offer him.

Mom went to the supermarket yesterday, but she has to go again today. Usually one trip lasts us a whole week.

Also, you could have warned us about his poop.

It smells awful! Mom says even little puppies are trained to go outside, and this dragon looks quite old, so why is he pooping on the carpet in her bedroom?

But I can see why you like him. When he's being sweet, he really is very sweet. He has a nice expression, doesn't he? And I like the funny snoring noise he makes when he's asleep.

Are you having a good time at the beach? Is the sun shining? Are you swimming a lot?

It's raining here.

Love from your favorite nephew,

Eddie

P.S. The smell of burning was the curtains. I put out the fire with a saucepan full of water. Luckily, they had dried by the time Mom saw them.

From: Edward Smith–Pickle

To: Morton Pickle

Date: Monday, August 1

Subject: The fridge

📎 **Attachments:** The hole

Dear Uncle Morton,

I wish I could say things were better with the dragon today, but actually, they're worse. This morning, we came downstairs for breakfast

and found he'd made a hole in the door of the fridge. I don't know why he couldn't just open it like everyone else. He drank all the milk and ate yesterday's leftover mac and cheese.

Mom was furious. I had to beg her and beg her and beg her to give him one more chance.

"I've already given him one last chance," she said. "Why should I give him another?"

I promised to help clean up any more of his messes. I think that was what changed her mind.

I'm hoping he'll go in the yard from now on.

Mom is keeping a tab for you. So far, you owe us two weeks of groceries and a new fridge. She says she'll charge you for the carpet, too, if she can't get the stains out.

I sent you two e-mails yesterday. Didn't you get either of them?

Eddie

From: Edward Smith-Pickle

To: Morton Pickle

Date: Monday, August 1

Subject: Your dragon again

📎 **Attachments:** Poop close-up

You might have to change your flights after all, Uncle M. Your dragon's pooped in the house, again. This time, he couldn't get into Mom's room, because she's been keeping her door shut, so he left it on the landing right outside. I scrubbed it with bleach, but there's still a stain on the carpet. I just hope Mom won't see it. If she does, she'll call the zoo right away. I know she will.

E

Dear Uncle Morton,

What's a tether?

I don't know and Mom won't tell me, but she's at the end of hers.

That's what she says anyway.

It was the curtains that did it.

Mom saw them last night. She was furious, but I managed to calm her down. I said I'd pay for new ones out of my allowance.

I don't actually have any money saved from my allowance, but I promised to start saving immediately.

Also, I pointed out that the hole in the curtains was really quite small.

Mom gave a big sigh and shrugged her shoulders. She stood on a chair and turned the curtains around so you could hardly see the hole. Not unless you were looking for it anyway. And why would anyone get down on the floor and search for holes at the edge of the curtain?

Then, this morning, the dragon breathed all over them again.

It was really quite dramatic. The whole room filled with smoke. While I was running back and forth with a pot full of water (six times!), your dragon just sat on the sofa. I wasn't expecting an apology, but he could at least have looked embarrassed.

Also, he knows he's not allowed on the sofa.

This is my fifth e-mail to you, Uncle M, and you haven't replied to one of them. I know you're on vacation, but even so, could you reply ASAP? Even if you can't come and collect your dragon, some tips on looking after him would be very much appreciated!

Eddie

P.S. If you don't know what ASAP means, it means As Soon As Possible.

P.P.S. Your tab so far: 3 loads of groceries, 2 curtains, 1 fridge, 1 rabbit, 1 new carpet. (Mom saw the stain.)

From: Edward Smith-Pickle

To: Morton Pickle

Date: Tuesday, August 2

Subject: Where are you?!!???

📎 **Attachments:** Mom on the rampage

Dear Uncle Morton,

Mom called your hotel. They said you never arrived. They said you canceled your reservation, and they gave your room to someone else.

So, where are you?

Mom says you've been lying to us. She says you've always told lies, even when you were a boy, and she was stupid to think you might have changed.

I didn't know what to say, Uncle Morton. I was sure you hadn't lied to us. I don't believe you're a liar. But if you're not staying at the Hotel

Splendide, why did you give us that number?
Where *are* you staying?

I told Mom anything might have happened.
Maybe you banged your head and you don't
know who you are anymore. Maybe you're
in the hospital, covered in bandages, and no
one knows who to call. Maybe you've been
kidnapped. You're always talking about your

enemies. Do you need us to pay a ransom? I hope not, because your tab with Mom is already long enough.

Mom doesn't think you've been kidnapped. Or bumped your head. She says you're just a selfish pig and always have been, and once you've collected your dragon she never wants to see you again.

I'm sure she didn't mean it, Uncle M.

Little sisters are always saying stuff like that. Emily does, too. The next day, she's forgotten what she even said.

Mom's probably just like that, too.

But even so, I think you should call her ASAP.

Eddie

Dear Uncle Morton,

Mom is about to call the zoo. She's going to ask them to take the dragon away.

I tried to persuade her not to. But she said it was the dragon or her.

I said the zoo probably wouldn't want her.

She said I should be careful because I was treading on thin ice.

I don't know what she meant, but I didn't want to ask. She had that expression on her face. Do you know the one I mean? The one that says, "You'd better keep out of my way."

So I have.

E

From: Edward Smith–Pickle

To: Morton Pickle

Date: Tuesday, August 2

Subject: Don't worry!

📎 **Attachments:** Mom and the dragon

Dear Uncle Morton,

The zookeepers aren't coming. They thought Mom was joking.

When they realized she was serious, they thought she was crazy.

Finally, they hung up.

So she called the animal shelter, but they didn't believe her, either.

They said, "There's no such thing as dragons."

Mom said, "Come here if you want to see one."

That was when they hung up, too.

Now Mom doesn't know what to do. She's threatening to kick the dragon out to the street.

I said she couldn't just leave a poor defenseless dragon out in the street, where anything might happen to him.

"I've got to do something," she said, "or I really will go crazy. What if he bites the neighbors? What if he eats one of the twins?"

It's true, he could easily pull them out of their stroller. They live across the street, and they're only eight months old. With teeth like his, he could gobble them up in a moment. I know you said he'd never harm another living creature, but that wasn't true, was it? What about Jemima?

Uncle M, I must have written you ten messages by now. Could you please write back?

Eddie

From: Edward Smith-Pickle

To: Morton Pickle

Date: Wednesday, August 3

Subject: Maud

📎 **Attachments:** Cat attack; Mom chatting

Dear Uncle Morton,

You're not going to believe what's happened now. The dragon just attacked Mrs. Kapelski's cats again. This time the yard is full of fur, and the petunias have gone up in smoke.

It was the cats' own fault, I suppose, because they know they're not allowed in our yard. They came in anyway. They always do. They didn't see your dragon snoozing on the patio. They were rolling around on the grass when he woke up and jumped on them.

Tigger got away without any problem, but the dragon managed to grab Maud's tail in his jaws.

I saw it all through the window. I was banging on the glass, trying to make the dragon stop, but he didn't pay any attention. Finally, Maud

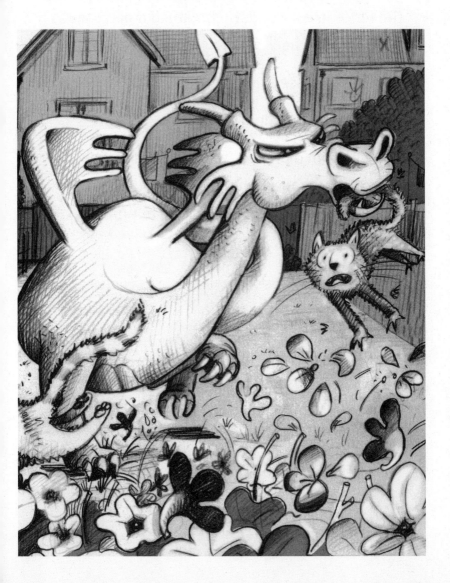

turned around and scratched him on the nose. The dragon wasn't expecting that! He was so surprised, he opened his jaws, and she was over the fence in a second. He breathed a great burst of flame after her.

Luckily, he missed.

Unluckily, he got Mom's petunias.

Luckily, Mom didn't see what happened. She was on the phone with the pet shop. She's been calling everyone she can think of, but no one wants a dragon.

Now she's sitting at the kitchen table with her head in her hands. She's run out of people to call. I haven't told her about the petunias yet, but she's going to see them soon, and then I don't know what will happen.

To be honest, Uncle M, I'm a bit worried about her. I asked about fixing the fridge, and Mom said, "What's the point? The dragon will just put another hole in it."

I suppose she's right, but even so, it would be good to have somewhere to keep the milk.

Eddie

P.S. You'll be glad to hear Maud is fine. She's still has her whole tail.

P.P.S. Your dragon has spent the rest of the morning picking fur out of his teeth. He won't be attacking any more cats in a hurry.

From: Edward Smith–Pickle

To: Morton Pickle

Date: Thursday, August 4

Subject: PLEASE READ THIS!!!!

Attachments: Mailman; Firefighters

Dear Uncle Morton,

I don't even know why I'm writing to you. You haven't answered any of my other e-mails. Maybe I've even got the wrong e-mail address, just like Mom had the wrong hotel. But I've got to tell someone what's happening, and I can't think of anyone else.

Today was the worst day so far. Your dragon set fire to the mailman.

To be fair to the dragon, I don't think he meant to. I think he must have been frightened by the letters coming through the mail slot. He breathed fire all over them. The flames went through the mail slot and out the other side, setting the mailman's sleeve on fire.

Luckily, the mailman wasn't hurt. Mom put the flames out with a blanket. But he's going to

need a new uniform, and he said he'll charge
us for it.

We had a lot of explaining to do. There was a big
fire engine parked outside the house and four

firefighters in our front yard, wanting to check our smoke alarms.

Mom told them about the dragon. She invited them in to see him.

The firefighters looked at one another in a funny way and backed down the front path.

When they'd gone, the mailman said he'd sue us. He said he'd report us to the police. He said we could expect never to get another letter in our lives. He said a lot more things that I didn't actually hear, because Mom put her hands over my ears.

Now Mom's upstairs in bed. She said she'll come downstairs to make dinner, but I don't know if she really will.

The dragon is lying on the sofa. I told him he should be ashamed of himself, but he doesn't look ashamed at all.

He won't get off the sofa, either. Not even when I shout at him. He knows he's not allowed on there.

Eddie

From: Edward Smith-Pickle

To: Morton Pickle

Date: Thursday, August 4

Subject: Postcard?

Attachments: The stamp

Dear Uncle M,

I've just been through what's left of our mail and found a postcard with a foreign stamp. Unfortunately, there was nothing else left, just the corner with the stamp on it, but I think the picture might have been of a beach. Did you send it to us? If you did, that's very nice of you, but it would be even nicer if you would answer my e-mails.

E

Dear Uncle Morton,

I am a long way past the end of my tether.

Yesterday I didn't think things could get any worse, but they just have.

Mom is upstairs again. She says she's not coming down till the dragon's gone. I said that might not be for three more days, and she said, "Then I'm going to be spending a lot of time in bed. You'd better find me some good books."

Emily and I haven't had any breakfast, and it looks as if we're not going to get any lunch, either.

Your dragon is in the kitchen. The door's shut. He won't let me in. I just tried, but he breathed a little bit of smoke in my direction. From the expression in his eyes, I could see it was a warning.

I'm not a coward, Uncle M, but I'm not stupid, either. I ran straight out and slammed the door behind me.

I waited for a few minutes, then I peered through the keyhole and saw what he'd done.

He's been through the cupboards, ripping off the doors and pulling out all the food. He's ripped open the packages. He's chewed through the cans. There's rice and lentils and spaghetti all over the kitchen floor.

Uncle Morton, what am I supposed to do?

Eddie

From: Morton Pickle

To: Edward Smith-Pickle

Date: Friday, August 5

Subject: Chocolate

Have you tried chocolate?

From: Edward Smith-Pickle

To: Morton Pickle

Date: Friday, August 5

Subject: Re: Chocolate

What do you mean, have I tried chocolate?

Of course I have! I love chocolate.

I don't want to be rude, Uncle Morton, but I'm beginning to worry that Mom might be right about you. I've been sending you e-mails for almost a whole week now and I've been begging you to answer and when you finally do, you just ask if I've ever tried chocolate.

Maybe you really have banged your head!

Have you?

If not, then why haven't you answered any of my other e-mails? Where have you been? And when are you going to come and collect your dragon?

Eddie

From: Morton Pickle

To: Edward Smith-Pickle

Date: Friday, August 5

Subject: Re: Re: Chocolate

I mean, have you tried giving the dragon chocolate?

From: Edward Smith–Pickle

To: Morton Pickle

Date: Friday, August 5

Subject: Re: Re: Re: Chocolate

📎 **Attachments:** The chocoholic

It works!!!!!!!!!!!!!!

From: Edward Smith–Pickle

To: Morton Pickle

Date: Saturday, August 6

Subject: Re: Re: Re: Re: Chocolate

📎 **Attachments:** Our very own flamethrower

Dear Uncle Morton,

I'm sorry I haven't replied more quickly to tell you what happened, but I've been too busy feeding the dragon all the chocolate in the house and then going to the store to get some more.

The dragon is a changed beast.

Mom says he's been behaving like a little angel, and he has. He's stopped stealing food. He poops on the grass. He doesn't even sit on the sofa anymore. Actually, that's not quite true, but he gets off as soon as he's told to.

Tonight we had a barbecue in our backyard. Your dragon lit the grill.

Then he ate six hot dogs, three hamburgers, and nine ears of corn. Luckily, Mom had just been to the supermarket, so there was enough for us, too.

Now your dragon is lying on the floor, looking up at me with his big eyes. I know I shouldn't give him any more chocolate. But I'm just going to give him one more piece and then it's time for bed.

Eddie

From: Edward Smith-Pickle

To: Morton Pickle

Date: Saturday, August 6

Subject: Re: Re: Re: Re: Re: Chocolate

Attachments: Storytime; Emily's new best friend

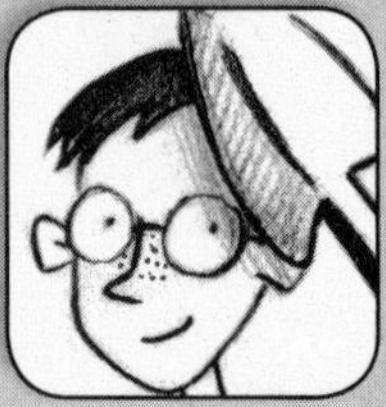

Dear Uncle Morton,

I thought you might like to know your dragon has now eaten:

12 bars of milk chocolate
14 bars of dark chocolate
6 Twix bars
1 Crunch bar
23 boxes of malted milk balls

The man at the store is starting to look at me in a funny way.

I thought Mom would mind buying so much candy, but she said, "If he's happy, I'm happy."

He is. Very.

Even Emily has forgiven him. She seems to have forgotten all about Jemima. I think she'd like to have your dragon as a pet instead.

She's even started calling him Cupcake.

I've told her several times that Cupcake isn't a suitable name for a dragon, but she doesn't seem to care.

Does he actually have a name?

If he doesn't, I would suggest Desolation. Or Firebreath. Or something like that.

But not Cupcake.

I hope you're enjoying the last few hours of your vacation and managing to get in a last swim and some sunshine. It's raining here.

See you tomorrow. Don't miss your flight!

Love,

Eddie

From: Morton Pickle

To: Edward Smith-Pickle

Date: Saturday, August 6

Subject: Re: Re: Re: Re: Re: Re: Chocolate

Attachments: My island; Hotel Bellevue; Les Fruits de Mer d'Alphonse

Hi Eddie,

Very glad to hear that my tip about chocolate did the trick. It always does with dragons, even the biggest of them. I remember hiking through the mountains of Outer Mongolia with a backpack almost entirely stuffed with candy bars. Without it, I wouldn't be here today. I fed it all to the biggest dragon I've ever seen in my life, a bad-tempered one with teeth as big as my hands and terrible breath.

I'll tell you the whole story when I see you, but I

don't have time now. I've got to be quick. I'm in the airport and my flight leaves any minute. But I wanted to write to you and say I AM SO VERY SORRY for not reading your messages earlier in the week. I could have checked my e-mail at the hotel, but I had resolved not to interrupt my vacation. That was stupid of me, I know, and I am exceedingly apologetic. I only looked yesterday because I had heard a rumor from a fellow guest that there has been terrible flooding in Lower Bisket, the town opposite my island. I have several good friends living there, so I wanted to check that they were safe. (You'll be glad to know

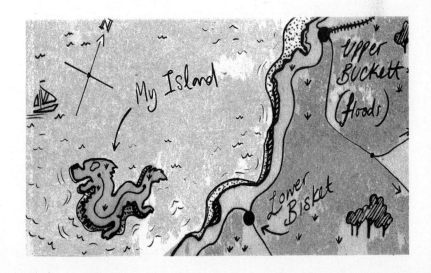

that the floods were actually in Upper Buckett, which is quite different.)

I'm very sorry, too, that my naughty little dragon has been behaving so badly. Were my instructions no use at all? I was quite sure I had included the tip about chocolate.

Will you please apologize to your mother about the mix-up over hotels? I had been planning to stay at the Hotel Splendide, which is why your mother had that address and phone number. On arrival, I discovered that the chef, the famous Alphonse Mulberry, had quarreled with the owner and moved to an establishment in the next town along the coast. So I moved there, too. I'm glad I did. His cooking is even more spectacular than I had remembered.

For some reason, I don't appear to have your mother's e-mail address, which is why I'm sending this to you. Please apologize to her on my behalf. I have bought her an enormous chunk

of Roquefort as a present. I know how much she likes cheese.

They're calling my flight. I'd better go and get on line. I'll see you very soon.

Lots of love from your affectionate and apologetic uncle,

Morton

From: Edward Smith-Pickle

To: Morton Pickle

Date: Monday, August 8

Subject: Au revoir

Attachments: Mom and her hose

Dear Uncle Morton,

I hope you had a good journey home. Did the dragon behave himself on the train?

Mom put up the new curtains, and she's ordered another fridge from the store. She says she never liked the petunias, and she's decided to plant roses instead. She's going to spend the rest of your money on new carpeting for all our bedrooms.

She loves the cheese, by the way.

I don't. It smells awful. Sorry for saying so, but it does.

Emily says thank you for the stuffed monkey. She

says he's almost as good as Jemima. I think he's even better. At least he doesn't need to be fed. Also, he can sleep in her bed instead of that cage in the backyard.

And thanks very much for the books. They'll be really useful if I ever learn French.

You know your list of instructions? Well, Mom finally found it behind the sofa. We've read it now. You did say the thing about chocolate, and lots of other useful stuff, too. If only we'd found the list before!

Mom says she thinks you just put the list there when you came to collect the dragon, but I told her not to be so silly.

Mrs. Kapelski's cats have started coming into the yard again. Mom chased them out with a hose. She said, "I wish that dragon was still here." Then she looked at me very quickly and said, "I don't really."

But I think she does.

I do, too.

He made everything very difficult, but he was fun, too.

I hope you're having a good time back home on your island.

By the way, when I said I'd like to visit, I really did mean it.

Will you send an official invitation to Mom? Otherwise, she's never going to let me.

Emily would like to come too, but I told her she's too young. She is, isn't she? She might fall off a cliff or something.

Lots of love from your favorite nephew,

Eddie

P.S. Please give Ziggy a chocolate bar from me.

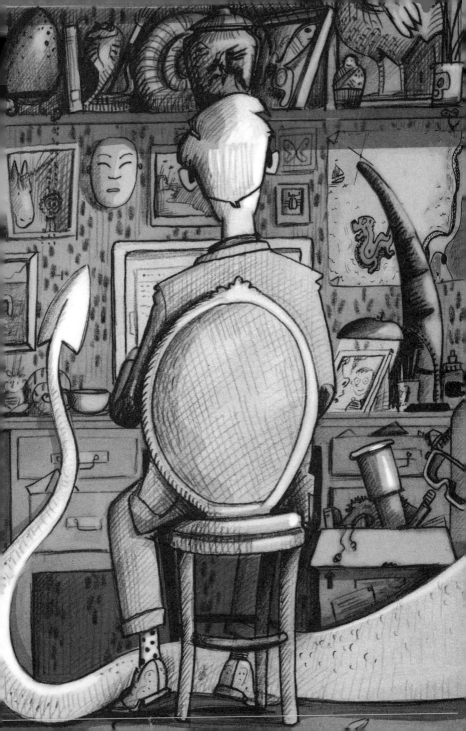

What's next for Eddie & Ziggy?

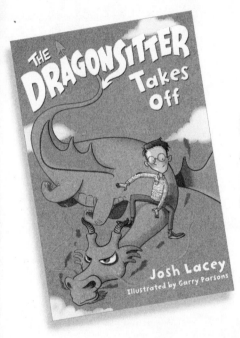

Don't miss their second adventure!

Turn the page for a sneak peek.
COMING SOON

Dear Uncle Morton,

I know you don't want to be disturbed, but I have to tell you some very bad news.

Ziggy has disappeared.

Mom says he was asleep on the carpet when she went to bed, but this morning he was nowhere to be seen.

I'm really sorry, Uncle Morton. We've only been looking after him for one night, and he's run away already.

He must hate being here.

Actually, he did seem depressed when you dropped him off. I bought him a box of malted milks balls as a present, but he didn't eat a single one.

I've been reading your notes. There's lots of useful information about mealtimes and clipping his claws, but nothing about what to do if he disappears.

Should we be searching for him, Uncle Morton? If so, where?

Eddie

Dear Uncle Morton,

We're back from school and Ziggy still isn't here.

While we were walking home, Emily said she saw him having a snack in the café.

I was already running to fetch him when she yelled, "Just kidding!"

I don't know why she thinks she's funny, because she's really not.

Mom called Mr. McDougall. He said he would row to your island first thing tomorrow morning and look for Ziggy. He can't go now because there's a storm.

I'll let you know as soon as we hear from him.

Eddie

Dear Uncle Morton,

Don't worry about my other two emails. We have found Ziggy.

He was in the linen closet. I suppose he'd crawled in there because it's nice and warm.

Mom was actually the one who found him. You would have thought she'd be pleased, but, in fact, she was furious. She said she didn't want a dirty dragon messing up her clean sheets. She grabbed him by the nose and tried to pull him out. He didn't like that at all. Luckily, Mom moved fast or he would have burned her hand off.

I think she's going to charge you for repainting

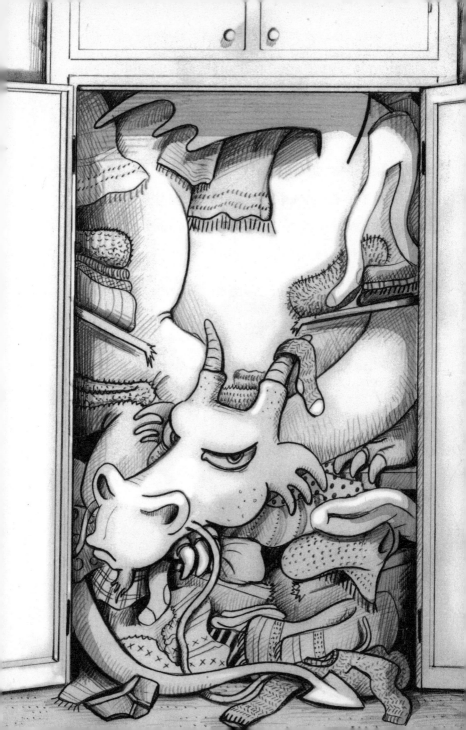

the wall. There's a big brown patch where he scorched the paint.

I still think he might be depressed.

We had mac and cheese for dinner. I saved some for Ziggy and left it outside the linen closet. When I checked just now, he hadn't even touched it.

But at least he's here and not wandering the streets.

Love,

Eddie

From: Edward Smith-Pickle

To: Morton Pickle

Date: Tuesday, October 18

Subject: Ziggy

📎 **Attachments:** Show-and-tell

Dear Uncle Morton,

I just wanted to tell you nothing has changed.

Ziggy won't move from the linen closet.

He still hasn't eaten a thing. Not even one malted milk ball.

I'm really quite worried about him.

To be honest, I'm also a bit annoyed, because I had been planning to take him to school today.

When I told Miss Brackenbury why I hadn't brought anything for show-and-tell, she just laughed and said I could do it next week instead.

I hope Ziggy will have come out of hiding by then.

Eddie

From: Morton Pickle

To: Edward Smith–Pickle

Date: Wednesday, October 19

Subject: Re: Ziggy

📎 **Attachments:** The yoga retreat

Hi Eddie,

Sorry I haven't replied earlier, but we're forbidden from using any electronic devices at the retreat.

I have sneaked down to the village to read my mail.

Please tell your mother that I'm very sorry about her linens and will, of course, buy her a new set of everything. And don't worry about Ziggy's appetite: If he gets hungry, he will eat.

Thanks again for looking after him. I would never have been able to come here otherwise.

The retreat is exhausting and strangely wonderful. We are woken at five o'clock in the morning and spend four hours sitting in silence before breakfast. The rest of the day is devoted to yoga, pausing only for a meal of vegetable curry and rice. My mind is clear and my body contorts into shapes that would have been impossible only last week.

Love from your affectionate uncle,

Morton

Dear Uncle Morton,

Are you sure Ziggy is a boy?

I think he might be a girl.

I mean, I think *she* might be a girl.

You're probably wondering why I'm thinking this, and the answer is very simple.

She has laid an egg in the linen closet.

Now I understand why she likes being in there. Not only is it nice and warm, but she's built herself a nest from Mom's clean sheets and towels.

The egg is green and shiny and about the size of a bike helmet.

Do you think I could take it to school next week for show-and-tell?

I promise I won't drop it.

Ziggy still isn't eating. Mom says she was ravenous when she was pregnant with me and Emily, but maybe dragons are different.

Eddie

Dear Uncle Morton,

There is a tiny crack in the egg. I'm sure it wasn't there yesterday.

Mom says I have to go to school, but I don't want to. What if the baby comes when I'm not here?

She's calling me. I've got to go.

It's so unfair!

If you get this, please, please, please will you call Mom and tell her someone needs to stay with the egg?

E

Dear Uncle Morton,

I'm glad to say the baby hasn't arrived yet.

When Mom picked us up and brought us home, I went straight upstairs to the linen closet.

The egg was still there.

It has changed, though. It's covered in more cracks.

Also, it keeps shaking and shuddering as if something is stirring under the surface.

I'm not going to sleep tonight.

Eddie

KEEP READING
for more from
Uncle Morton!

Instructions for Dragonsitting

Ziggy has an excellent appetite and will happily snack all day long, but I try to restrict his mealtimes to the same as mine.

He will eat anything except curry and porridge.

Please don't give him ice cream. It wreaks havoc with his digestion. He does love it, though, so don't leave any within reach.

Don't forget: Dragons will do anything for chocolate! I usually keep several bars of milk and dark chocolate for emergencies.

Ziggy isn't an energetic creature. He usually sleeps all night and most of the day, and requires only a little gentle exercise. If he's feeling restless, he'll take himself for a quick flight and be home in time for dinner.

I usually let him outside to do his business after breakfast and before bedtime. Accidents will happen, and I shall, of course, compensate you for any damage.

He is perfectly happy curling up anywhere, even on the hardest cold stone floor, but will be grateful for a couple of cushions. Please don't let him sleep in your bed—I don't want him getting into bad habits.

I have clipped his claws, so you shouldn't need to. If you do, I recommend garden shears.

If his rash recurs, call Isobel Macintyre, our vet in Lower Bisket. See the other sheet for her number. She knows Ziggy well and could help in a crisis.

If you have a nonmedical emergency, try Mr. McDougall.

Thanks again for looking after Ziggy. See you soon.

M

Dear Miss Brackenbury,

Thank you so much for your delightful e-mail. There was no need to introduce yourself; Eddie has told me how much he enjoys your lessons, which, I can assure you, is a great compliment from my nephew.

I'm touched and flattered by your suggestion that I visit the school and give a talk about my travels. I have indeed been to some extraordinary places, and I always enjoy chatting about the months I spent tagging penguins in Patagonia or my voyage in a leaky canoe down the farthest tributaries of the Amazon.

However, I chose some years ago to come and live

on a small island, just off the coast of Scotland, and I have many duties here. I am also, I must confess, a nervous public speaker, and your students would probably be bored by my ramblings.

Instead of myself, may I offer a copy of my book? It will be published by a small press later this year—the title is: *The Winged Serpents of Zavkhan: In Search of the Dragons of Outer Mongolia.*

I shall send a couple of copies to Eddie and ask him to bring one to school. You might like to read a few pages to your class. Obviously, I wouldn't want to encourage schoolchildren to hunt for dragons—they are quiet creatures and prefer to be left alone—but I should like to inspire in the younger generation a respect for wildlife and a longing for adventure.

With all best wishes,

Morton

THE DRAGONSITTER Series

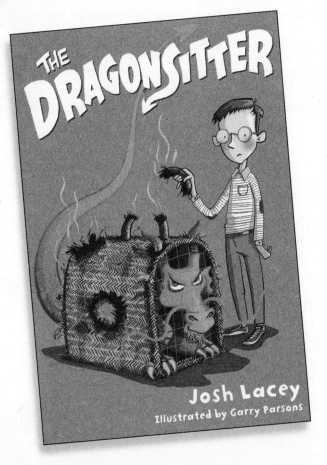

COMING APRIL 2016

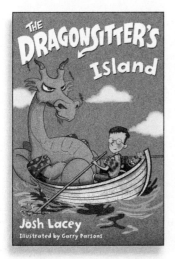

COMING OCTOBER 2016

COLLECT THEM ALL!

If you enjoyed THE DRAGONSITTER, you might also like these series, available now!

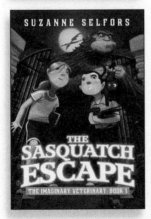

Don't miss a single **SPACE TAXI** adventure!

BOOK 1

BOOK 2

BOOK 3

BOOK 4

Meet
LOLA LEVINE

Second-grader Lola Levine loves writing in her *diario* and playing soccer with her team, the Orange Smoothies. But when a soccer game during recess gets "too competitive," Lola accidentally hurts her classmate Juan Gomez. Now everyone is calling her Mean Lola Levine! What will Lola do?

COMING SOON

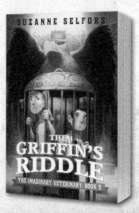

About the Author

JOSH LACEY is the author of many books for children, including *The Island of Thieves*, *Bearkeeper*, and the Grk series. He worked as a journalist, a teacher, and a screenwriter before writing his first book, *A Dog Called Grk*. Josh lives in London with his wife and daughters.

About the Illustrator

GARRY PARSONS has illustrated several books for children and is the author and illustrator of *Krong!*, winner of the Perth and Kinross Picture Book Award. Garry lives in London.